THE FIGHT FOR THE GLEN

THE FIGHT FOR THE GLEN

By
Curtis Colby

Illustrations by
Joseph Bergeron

EMC Corporation
St. Paul, Minnesota

Library of Congress Cataloging in Publication Data

Colby, Curtis.
   The fight for the Glen.

   (His Adventures in the Glen)
   SUMMARY: Children try to save the wooded area
near their home from being turned into a shopping
center.
   [1. Environmental protection—Fiction]
I.   Bergeron, Joseph R., illus.   II.   Title.
PZ7.C6724Fi   [Fic]   73-14586
ISBN 0-88436-027-4
ISBN 0-88436-028-8 (pbk.)

Published by EMC Corporation
180 East Sixth Street
St. Paul, Minnesota 55101
Printed in the United States of America
0987654321

ADVENTURES IN THE GLEN SERIES

Laura came bursting into the house. She was out of breath from running in the summer heat.

"They're going to spoil the Glen!" she cried.

Her twin brother Dave was listening to records. He turned down the record player. "They're going to what?" he asked.

Laura caught her breath. "I was sitting by the pond," she said, "and I heard some men talking. They want to build a shopping center in the Glen!"

"You're kidding!"

"I'm not kidding. They want to build it around the pond. It would be the world's most beautiful shopping center. That's what one man kept saying. The stores would be spread out. There would be grass and trees between them. The man said it was a whole new idea. He wants to call it a shopping park."

The Glen now was mostly woodland. In one part, a creek ran into a large pond. The pond, at its lower end, turned into a swamp.

All around the Glen were houses and stores. But up to now, the Glen had been left alone.

The Glen was a home for ducks and Canada geese. An otter lived there. So did a raccoon. Muskrats built their houses there. There were squirrels and rabbits in the woods. Hawks and owls nested in the trees.

"We can't let them ruin it!" said Laura. "We have to do something!"

"What?" Dave wondered.

Their mother was listening. "Why don't you ask your father when he comes home?" she said.

The twins' father was a lawyer. Mr. Jackson listened carefully when Laura told him what she had heard.

"It sounds to me," he said, "like it is just an idea. Those men were only talking about what they would *like* to do."

"But suppose they go ahead and do it?" asked Dave.

"It would cost them a lot of money," said Mr. Jackson. "They would have to fill in the swamp. Then they would have to find another place for the water to go. Now all the extra water goes into the swamp. The whole thing would be a big deal. That's why nobody has built anything in the Glen yet. It would cost too much."

"Do they just care about the money?" asked Laura. "Doesn't anybody care about the wildlife?"

"I think the people who live around here do," her father said. "To them the Glen has become a kind of nature reserve. But they don't own it."

"Who does own the Glen?" Dave asked.

"That's a good question," said Mr. Jackson. "Different people may own different parts of it. Some parts may even be owned by the state. I can find out. In fact, I think I will. I would like to know who owns that land. But don't worry about the shopping center. I bet they will find it costs too much to build."

Dave wouldn't give up. "What if they do try to build it?" he wanted to know.

"Then," said his father, "your best hope is that a lot of people make a big fuss. If enough people wanted to save the Glen they could do it."

The next morning the twins met their friends, Bill and Tony. They told the boys about the shopping center.

"Maybe your father is right," Tony said. "Maybe nothing will happen."

"But we shouldn't take any chances," said Bill. "I'm going to hang around the Glen a lot this summer."

"Me too," said Dave. "We should keep a lookout for what's going on."

They didn't have long to wait. They were all camping overnight in the Glen a few days later. In the morning they saw two men near the pond. The men were wearing work clothes and boots. One man was looking at a map. The other was writing on a pad of paper.

PROPERTY OF
GAGE SCHOOL

"Are those the same men?" Dave asked Laura.

"No. The ones I saw looked like businessmen."

"I'm going to ask these guys what they're doing," said Tony.

"They won't tell you," said Bill.

"Why not? I'm only a kid. They won't think *I* know anything. I'll take my fishing rod."

Tony walked down to the pond. He baited his hook and cast out. The men looked at him.

"Hi, Mister," Tony said to the man with the map. "What are you doing?"

"Looking around a little, that's all," the man said. "What do you catch out of here?"

"Catfish mostly," said Tony. "Sometimes a trout."

The man turned to his partner. "It would be nice for the kids," he said. "They could fish while their mothers shop."

"Shop?" said Tony. "Where would people shop?"

"Well, we might just build a place for them to shop."

"Here? That would be neat!" Tony said. "But there's so much swamp. And in the hilly places, the woods are pretty thick. How can you build anything?"

The man laughed. "That's what we're figuring out now," he said. "I think we can do it. We have some big machines. You would be surprised what we can do. We can take land like this and make it into anything you want."

"Wow!" said Tony. "Are you the one who's going to do it?"

The man laughed again. "Me and a few hundred other guys," he said.

"Can I come and watch? When are you going to do it?"

"Sure you can watch. We might even start before you go back to school. And if you see me around, you just holler. I'll give you a ride on the biggest bulldozer you ever saw."

The two men walked off toward the swamp. Tony suddenly felt hollow inside. Bulldozers in the Glen. Even before school started, maybe. This was more than just an idea!

18

That afternoon, the four friends went to the twins' house. Tony and Bill were invited to stay for supper.

When Mr. Jackson came home, he had some news too. He had found out who owned the land. Most of it was state land. He had found out something else, too. A big company was trying to buy the land. The company had a lot of money to build a shopping center in the Glen.

"Well, we know what's happening," said Dave. "Now we have to decide what to do."

Mr. Jackson saw Tony frowning. "Maybe Tony has an idea," he said.

Tony looked up. "No," he said. "I wasn't thinking about that. I was thinking about the man I talked to at the pond today."

"What about him?" asked Mr. Jackson.

"Well, I was putting on an act with him and everything. But he really wasn't a bad guy. He is just doing his job. He doesn't think he will hurt the Glen. He thinks he is going to make it a better place."

"So what should we do?" said Laura. "Let him spoil it, just because he's a nice guy doing his job?"

"That isn't what I said!" Tony exploded. "I care about the Glen as much as you do!"

"Whoa. Hold on," said Mr. Jackson. "Tony has a point. There are no bad guys and good guys in something like this. In fact, the kind of shopping center they are planning sounds pretty good."

"We have enough shopping centers around here," Laura said.

Her father looked at her. "What if people don't think so?" he asked. "What if they would rather have the shopping center than the Glen?"

Laura didn't say anything.

Bill spoke up. "It seems to me," he said, "the first step is to let people know what's going on."

"That's the idea," said Mr. Jackson. "That's what bothers me about this whole thing. They are going ahead without telling anybody. The Glen is mostly state land. That means it is public land. The public has a right to know. And the public should decide."

"Let's write it all out on paper," said Dave. "We can make copies. Then we'll put them in people's mailboxes."

"That's a lot of work, Dave," said his father.

"We can do it," Dave said.

"All right," said Mr. Jackson. "I'll get copies made if you will take them around. Let's figure out what you want to say."

They argued over the words for a long time. At last they agreed on a short statement:

Dave and Laura and Bill and Tony got their friends to help. A copy of the statement went into every mailbox they could find. Some mothers passed out copies at supermarkets.

Copies were sent to newspapers and TV and radio stations. A local newspaper had a story about the Glen. People who had never been there came to see it. State officials began getting letters about it.

Meetings were held. The big company sent men to the meetings. They told how beautiful the shopping center would look. Some people said it would be a good thing. Other people said they didn't need another shopping center. They liked the Glen the way it was.

Bill and Tony and the twins went to one of the meetings. They were surprised at all the shouting.

"Wow!" said Bill. "We really started something."

Mr. Jackson spoke against the shopping center at the meeting. After the meeting, Laura asked him what would happen.

"I don't know," he said. "Most people seem to be on our side. But you heard them in there. Some people really want the shopping center. And some don't care one way or the other."

Nothing was decided at the meetings. People just argued. But the arguments made news. Television cameramen went to a meeting. They also went to the Glen. Local stations reported the story on the evening news.

State officials became worried. They had agreed to sell the land to the company. Now they were not so sure. They decided to wait before doing anything.

Meanwhile, people kept coming to the Glen. State lawmakers had their pictures taken by the pond. Conservation officials sloshed through the swamp. By the end of summer, most of the wildlife was hiding.

"There are too many people," Tony complained.

"People are better than bulldozers," said Laura.

"And they'll help save the Glen," added Dave.

Dave was right. That winter the lawmakers met in the state capital. They passed a law making the Glen a state park.

The fight was over. The Glen had won.

Soon afterward, a reporter came to see Bill and Tony and the twins. He was going to write a final news story about the Glen.

"I hear you kids are the ones who started this whole thing," the reporter said. "Why did you go to all the trouble?"

"Because the Glen is worth it," said Laura. "There are lots of places to build a shopping center. But you can't find many places like the Glen anymore."

The reporter smiled as he wrote this down. "You have just given me the ending for my story," he said.